Surprise!

Surprise!

Adapted by Laurie McElroy

Based on "Josh Runs into Oprah," written by Ethan Benville,
and "Vicious Tiberius," written by George Doty IV

Based on *Drake & Josh* created by Dan Schneider

SCHOLASTIC INC.

New York   Toronto   London   Auckland   Sydney
Mexico City   New Delhi   Hong Kong   Buenos Aires

ISBN-13: 978-0-439-91645-5
ISBN-10: 0-439-91645-3

12 11 10 9 8 7 6 5 4 3 2   7 8 9 10 11/0

Printed in the U.S.A.
First printing, August 2007

NICKELODEON

Drake & Josh

Surprise!

Part One:
Josh Runs into Oprah

Prologue

Josh Nichols sat at his desk and checked his e-mail before launching into his history homework. "Get this," he said. "Drake says I have bad luck." Clearly Josh didn't agree.

Drake Parker always put food before homework. He sat at the kitchen table spreading peanut butter on a slice of bread. "I say Josh has bad luck." he said. "You know why?"

Josh shook his head. "I do not have bad luck."

"Because he has bad luck." Drake said matter-of-factly. He grabbed the jelly container and squeezed.

"Anytime something terrible happens to me, it's because of Drake," Josh said, throwing his arms up into the air. That wasn't bad luck. That was having a brother who created disasters all over the place.

"But Josh blames all his problems on me." Drake said. Drake didn't get it. All he ever did was try to help Josh out and bring some excitement to his life.

Josh listed the evidence. "Like, why did I get food poisoning?" he asked. "Because Drake forgot to refrigerate the clams." He grimaced, remembering how sick he was.

Drake couldn't believe the bad rap he was getting. "He gives me no credit for the nice stuff I do for him," he said. Drake spread the jelly on a second piece of bread and closed his sandwich.

Josh wasn't finished. "Why do I have foot burns?" he asked, pulling his leg up into the air and wriggling his sneaker. "Because Drake accidentally set my socks on fire."

Drake had evidence, too, and he wanted credit for the nice things he did for Josh. "Like his desk lamp," he said. "It was flickering, right? So I fixed the switch."

"Well, I'd better get started on my homework," Josh said. He reached out to turn on his desk lamp. *Bzzzzt!* The lamp flickered and buzzed. Josh sputtered and shook along with it as electricity ran through his body.

Drake got ready to take a big bite of his **PB&J** sandwich. "I just think Josh needs to appreciate me a little more, you know?" Drake said, convinced he was in the right. "Because if you ask me, his life is way more fun when I'm around."

Josh couldn't answer. He was too busy buzzing and twitching and sputtering. The hair on the top of his head started to stand up.

"I'm not asking for, like, a pat on the back every day," Drake said between bites. "But I just think he could give me a little more credit now and then. You know? I mean, come on." Drake took another bite, wondering if Josh had even noticed that Drake fixed his desk lamp.

The lamp flickered one last time while Josh continued to twitch and shudder. Finally, he fell over on his side and broke contact with the lamp.

Had he been able to speak, he would have said, "See, case closed." But he couldn't pry his lips apart.

The lights flickered in the kitchen, but Drake didn't notice. He swallowed half a glass of orange juice. It went great with his **PB&J**. "Mmm," he said. "I like juice."

CHAPTER ONE

Josh's friends Craig and Eric tiptoed into the bedroom Josh shared with Drake. Josh was sound asleep, facedown, snoring into his pillow. Craig and Eric stood on either side of his bed and launched into a song they had written themselves.

> *For it's your happy good birthday,*
> *For it's your happy good birthday,*
> *For it's your happy good birthday,*
> *Happy Birthday to you, Josh!*

Josh jumped up, startled, confused, and half asleep. Then a grin crept across his face. "Oh, you guys remembered!" He checked his alarm clock, surprised they had come early enough to wake him up. "Wow, it's early."

"Yeah, we were heading down to the botanical garden center," Eric explained. "On Saturdays they let you in for half price if you get there before nine."

"Petunias, here we come," Craig said, practically jumping up and down. He was way too excited about the whole idea of half-price flowers.

Craig wasn't the only one who got excited about things that most teenagers didn't exactly find thrilling. Eric remembered something — actually, someone — who could make Josh jump up and down with excitement: talk show host Oprah Winfrey. Josh was a huge fan, and Oprah was coming to San Diego to film a show.

"Did you get tickets to see Oprah?" Eric asked.

"No," Josh said, getting out of bed. Even though it was his birthday, he couldn't keep the disappointment out of his voice. He was totally bummed. "They were gone in, like, less than an hour." He couldn't believe Oprah was coming to town and he wasn't going to get to see her.

Eric tried to make Josh feel better. "Maybe she'll come back to San Diego again sometime."

"I doubt that," Craig said.

"No one needs your negativity," Eric snapped. What was Craig doing? It was Josh's birthday!

But Craig reacted to Eric's tone of voice. "You sang flat," he snapped back.

"You want a pop in the chops?" Eric said, making a fist.

Craig raised his fists too, ready to go at it.

Josh jumped between the two of them. "Guys, guys, guys! C'mon," he said. "No fighting on Joshie's birthday."

"He's right," Craig said with a grin. The whole thing was silly, anyway. "C'mon," he said. "Let's go see those petunias."

Josh raised an eyebrow, more awake now. Petunias?

Eric didn't have the same reaction. "Okay," he said with a smile.

They were headed out of the bedroom just as Drake was coming in, toweling his hair dry, already dressed in jeans and a logo T-shirt.

"Hi, Drake," Craig and Eric said at the same time.

"Who let you guys in our house?" Drake asked. Josh's geeky friends weren't exactly his favorite people.

"Megan opened the door," Craig said. "And told us that we could —"

Drake slammed the door in their faces, cutting Craig off.

Josh laughed. Craig and Eric never seemed to mind Drake's insults. They always came back for more.

"So . . ." Josh smiled, waiting for Drake to wish him a happy birthday. "How was your shower?"

Drake eyed his brother, confused. Since when did Josh care about his showers? "Fine," he said, but noticed that Josh was waiting for something more. "Wet," he added.

"How come you're up and dressed so early?" Josh asked, watching Drake search for something on his desk.

"Because today is a very special day," Drake announced.

Josh's grin got even bigger. *Drake must have something amazing planned for my birthday*, he thought, giggling. "Ohhhhh, I know," he said, scuffing his foot on the floor.

"Dude, check it out." Drake handed his brother a flyer.

Josh's face fell. "'Guitar World free giveaway,'" he read.

"Yeah, you see, the first fifty people who buy something from there get a free set of bongo drums," Drake said, drumming in the air.

"Oh," Josh said.

Drake didn't notice the disappointment in his brother's voice. "Yeah, and after that I'm going to pick up Tabitha and take her to lunch." Drake searched the desk some more and came up with his keys. "You know, things are getting pretty serious between me and her," he said thoughtfully.

Josh did a double take. "You've been dating her since Tuesday," he said sarcastically.

"I know," Drake said, surprised. Drake was popular with girls. If he went on more than one or two dates with just one girl, that equaled "serious" in his dating life. He grabbed the Guitar World flyer out of Josh's hand and headed out of the room, jiggling his keys. "See ya."

"Wait, wait, Drake," Josh said. Was Drake actually going to leave without wishing his brother a happy birthday?

"What?" Drake asked impatiently. He had to get to Guitar World.

"Isn't there something you want to say to me?" Josh asked with a smile.

Drake focused on his brother for a second, his hand on the doorknob. "Yeah, you have a little dried drool on your face there," he said, just before he closed the door behind him and ran down the stairs.

Josh stared at the door. His shoulders slumped. "He forgot my birthday," Josh said to himself. He and Drake had had their ups and downs, but Drake had never forgotten Josh's birthday before. Could he be so unimportant in his brother's life that bongo drums and girls he had known for just a few days got more attention?

Drake and Josh were two guys with two different — totally different — personalities. Going to the same school used to be the only thing they had in common, but that changed in a huge way when Drake's mom married Josh's dad. Drake and Josh were suddenly brothers — and roommates.

Drake wasn't what you would call happy about it at first. Drake was totally into having a good time —

playing his guitar and hanging with his friends. He wasn't exactly big on school — well, except for the girls — and he'd rather do anything than homework. He thought Josh was more than a little strange, in an especially geeky sort of way. And he had to share his supercool room — one of his favorite places to hang out, play his guitar, and think about girls — with Josh the supergeek.

Josh was totally into following the rules — all the rules. Teachers thought he was the greatest. Not only did he do all his homework and study for tests, Josh did extra-credit assignments, too. In other words, Josh didn't exactly hang out with the same high school in-crowd as Drake did. He hung with guys like Craig and Eric, who got excited about petunias.

But hanging out with his new stepbrother was one of Josh's favorite things to do. He loved the room they shared. It was unfinished with exposed beams and unpainted wallboard. Band posters, road signs, and old license plates hung on the walls. Drake had built him-self a loft bed, and added a great old sofa and comfy chairs he found at a yard sale.

Drake eventually learned to like having Josh around,

too. Now they were more than brothers — they were best friends. Or so Josh thought.

That's why Josh was totally bummed about Drake forgetting his birthday. He put a hand on his cheek and felt something sticky. "Oh, that is dried drool," he moaned, rubbing his face to get the disgusting stuff off.

CHAPTER TWO

Megan Parker, Drake and Josh's little sister, sat on the couch playing with an electronic toy. She worked the tiny computer with her thumbs, staring intently at the screen.

Josh heard high-pitched yips and barks when he wandered into the living room. "Hey, Megs," he said.

"Hey, Happy Birthday," Megan said with a smile.

"You remembered?" Josh asked. He couldn't believe it. Megan remembered his birthday. And was she actually being nice to him?

Usually the only thing Megan remembered was to call him a geek, or to shrink his underwear in the washing machine. His little sister looked like a normal girl, but she was an evil genius who gave new meaning to the word *troublemaker*. Unfortunately for her brothers, Megan was an expert at pulling pranks. She stopped at nothing to embarrass them.

"Of course," Megan said with a sweet smile. "Why wouldn't I?"

Josh flopped in a chair. "Drake forgot," he said. The fact that Megan did remember his birthday made it even worse that Drake didn't.

"And you're surprised?" Megan asked. "His brain's like a black hole. Stuff keeps getting sucked in and nothing ever comes out."

Josh laughed. Megan could be funny when she was making fun of someone else. "Yeah, I guess," he agreed.

"Here," Megan said, walking across the living room to the pass-through window that led to the kitchen. "I've got something that will cheer you up."

"What?" Josh couldn't believe it. Not only had Megan remembered his birthday but she had actually planned a surprise for him. He followed her.

Megan flipped her long dark hair over her shoulder and lifted the top off of a cake pan on the counter. "Ta-da!" she said with a flourish.

Underneath the cover was a beautiful birthday cake with the words *Happy Birthday, Josh* written on the white icing. Megan had even added a few candles and decorated the edges of the cake with fresh strawberries.

"You made me a birthday cake?" Josh asked with a big grin.

"Uh-huh," Megan said, lighting the candles. "Mom gave me the recipe. I think it came out pretty good."

"Wow," Josh said, leaning in to take a closer look. Then he remembered just who it was who made the cake. Megan was at her most dangerous when she was pretending to be nice. He whipped around. "It's full of poison, isn't it?"

Megan crossed her arms with a frown. "No."

"What then?" Josh asked, remembering some of Megan's food-related tricks and their painful results. "Hot sauce? Some kind of extreme laxative?"

"Oh, come on," Megan said seriously. "I wouldn't make you eat a cake that made you sick on your birthday."

The sad look on Megan's face made Josh feel bad about distrusting her. She was only trying to be nice to him on his birthday, and if it was Mom's recipe it had to be good. "I'm sorry," he said.

"It's okay," Megan said, turning him around so that he faced the cake again. "Now make a wish," she said.

"All right!" Josh closed his eyes and wished that

somehow he could get tickets to see Oprah. He took a deep breath and leaned in, opening his mouth wide to blow out the candles.

Ka-boom!

The cake blew up in his face, covering Josh, the kitchen, and the floor in cake and frosting. He slowly turned to Megan, opening his mouth to spit out the giant wad of cake that had landed there. To make things even worse, it didn't even taste good. And Josh was pretty sure who would get stuck cleaning the mess. Not Megan. Him.

Megan laughed and put her hand on her hip. "I didn't say it wouldn't explode."

"I don't blame you so much for doing it," Josh said slowly, peering at her through frosting-covered eyes, "as I blame myself for not anticipating it." Cake fell from his hair onto the carpet.

Megan's attention was drawn away by more yips coming from her game. "I've got to check on Toby," she said.

"Who's Toby?" Josh asked, walking into the kitchen to grab some napkins to wipe his face.

"He's a virtual pet," Megan answered. "I'm watching him for my friend Janie while she's at bassoon camp."

Josh came back into the living room, digging some cake out of his ear. "Why didn't she take Toby with her?"

"Because he's a lot of work," Megan explained, punching the buttons with her thumbs. "You have to feed him, walk him, groom him, and play with him or else he'll die."

"Cool!" Josh said. "Can I see it?"

"No!" Megan said, turning her back on her brother. "He doesn't like men." Then she turned to Josh with a disgusted look on her face. "Or whatever you are."

Josh just stared at his sister. Not only had she just blown up a cake in his face, now she was insulting him. And he had walked right into both of those things. When would he learn?

He heard a drumming sound coming from upstairs. "What is that?" he asked.

"Drake. He got back while you were in the kitchen. He's upstairs playing with his new bongos."

Bongos. Josh rolled his eyes. Bongos that were more

important to Drake than his own brother's birthday. "Him and those stupid hippie drums," Josh muttered.

Megan wasn't listening. Toby was barking like mad to go outside and Megan couldn't find his virtual leash.

"I'm going to go talk to him," Josh said.

"Okay," Megan answered. She didn't take her eyes off the small computer screen, but she wasn't fast enough. "Oh, Toby," she whined. "Not on the virtual couch!" She dropped the game on the coffee table as if the mess could come right through the computer screen.

Drake sat on the couch in his room beating on his bongo drums. He came to the end of a song. "Okay, name it," he said into the phone.

"'Zero Gravity.' Over My Thumb," said the voice on the other end.

"Yeah," Drake said. "All right, see if you can get this one." He launched into another song, using his fingers and the palms of his hands to drum the beat. He heard a squawk through the speakerphone.

"Trevor!"

Then Trevor's voice. "Hey, dude," he said. "I've got to clean my room or my mom's gonna kill me."

"Oh, okay," Drake said, putting the drums down.

Josh came into the room just in time to hear Drake finish his conversation.

"But don't forget," Drake told Trevor. "You've got to get to the Premiere early tonight for the party."

The Premiere was a local movie theater and café where Drake and Josh hung out. Josh worked there part-time, too. It was the perfect place for a surprise birthday party.

Drake hadn't forgotten! He was just pretending so that Josh wouldn't suspect anything. A huge grin spread across Josh's face. Drake was throwing Josh a party.

"Why early?" Trevor asked.

"Because it's a surprise," Drake answered. "We've got to get everything set up."

"Okay," Trevor said.

"Okay, later," Drake said, hanging up the phone.

Josh slammed the door, pretending that he hadn't heard Drake's party plans. "Hey," he said.

"Hey. What's up with the . . . ?" Drake said, pointing to Josh's cake-covered face and shirt.

"Megan," Josh said.

"Ah." Josh didn't need to say any more. Drake had been the victim of enough of Megan's pranks. A painful memory flashed across his mind, and then he changed the subject. "Hey, are you doing anything tonight?" he asked.

"Uh, no." Josh tried to look nonchalant so Drake wouldn't guess that he already knew about the surprise party. "No plans," he said. He tried to keep the big smile from creeping over his face again, but he couldn't.

"Good," Drake said. "Why don't you show up to the Premiere tonight around eight o'clock?"

"Uh, sure," Josh stammered.

"Cool, see you there," Drake said, heading out of the room. He stopped to run a finger down Josh's cheek and tasted the frosting.

Normally that was the kind of thing that drove Josh crazy. But not today. He jumped on the couch and grabbed Drake's new hippie drums.

"He remembered," Josh sang, banging on the drums. "My birthday."

He couldn't sing and drum at the same time, so he

punctuated each line of his new song with a few taps on the bongos.

"Drake's gonna throw me a big par-tay. I can't wait to go-oh."

Josh was too excited to care anymore about the exploding cake or what he might sound like. He launched into a drumbeat rhythm and couldn't stop.

Drake remembered his birthday!

CHAPTER THREE

Josh strolled into the Premiere a few minutes after eight o'clock. Kids milled around talking and laughing. Drake was tying *Happy Birthday* balloons to the railing around the café area.

Josh threw his arms out and used his best surprised face. "Hey, hey!" he yelled.

"Hey, Josh," some of the kids said in unison.

"Party!" Josh said, with a huge grin. "Hey, how are you, buddy?" he said, patting one guy on the shoulder. "Hey, Jess," Josh said, reaching out to shake the girl's hand. "Thanks for coming out. It means a lot."

Jess looked confused, but shook Josh's hand anyway.

Josh was too excited to notice. "Stevie!" Josh said, messing up Steve's hair. "You got your hair cut. I liked it better the old way, but you're a good guy."

Stevie watched Josh walk away. Why was he acting like a bad comic, he wondered.

But Josh had spotted Drake. He ran up to him and slapped him on the shoulder, then grabbed him in a big bear hug. Drake stared while Josh stepped back with a giggle. "Drake, man. I mean this party. It's really nice of you."

Drake's forehead wrinkled in confusion, but he didn't have time to ask Josh what he was babbling about. "Thanks," Drake said, turning back to the balloons.

"Yeah, I mean I almost thought you forgot my —"

Josh was cut off when a friend of Drake's ran in from outside. "She's coming in!" he yelled.

"Oh, everybody," Drake said. "Hide! Hide!"

The kids ducked behind tables, chairs, and video games.

Josh looked around. "Why is everybody hiding?" he asked. "I'm already here."

Drake grabbed Josh's arm and pulled his brother to the floor. Josh hit the ground with a loud thud.

Drake's lookout peeked around the corner. "Now!" he said in a loud whisper.

The kids jumped to their feet and shouted, "Surprise!" just as Tabitha walked into the Premiere.

"Oh my gosh!" Tabitha yelled. "How did you guys know it was my birthday?"

Drake stepped in front of her and opened his arms with a huge smile.

"Drake, you're the best," she said.

"Happy birthday, Tabitha," he said with a grin.

But he didn't get to savor the moment. Josh latched on to his brother's arm and pulled him away.

"Hey, what?" Drake asked, confused.

"You threw this whole surprise birthday party for *Tabitha*?" Josh asked. "A girl you met five days ago?"

"Well, yeah, why?" Drake asked, confused. What was Josh getting so worked up about?

Josh shook his head in disgust. It was becoming totally clear to him that Drake cared more about a girl who was practically a stranger than he did about his own brother. "Nothing," Josh muttered. "Forget it."

"Where are you going?" Drake asked. The party had just started and Josh was walking away.

"Home," Josh snapped.

"Who's that guy?" Tabitha asked, watching Josh leave.

"That was my brother, Josh," Drake said, still trying to make sense of Josh's weird behavior.

"Well, he's lucky, then," Tabitha said with a smile. "Because he's got the sweetest, most thoughtful brother in the whole entire world."

Helen, the manager of the Premiere and Josh's boss, walked up with a present in her hand. "Hey, do you know where Josh went?" she asked. "I want to give him this birthday present."

"Oh, no," Drake said, sure that Helen was mixed up. "It's Tabitha's birthday today."

"Oh, well, according to my clipboard it's Josh's birthday today, too."

"What?" Drake's jaw dropped.

Helen held out the clipboard so Drake could see her list of employees and their birthdays. "The clipboard does not lie," she said.

Drake's face fell. Suddenly Josh's weirder-than-usual behavior made total sense. "Oh my gosh," he said. "Tabitha, I've got to go fix something, okay?"

"Sure," Tabitha said, but Drake was already gone.

Helen still stood there holding Josh's present. "I

bought him one of those electric nose hair trimmers," she said to Tabitha.

"A nose hair trimmer?" Tabitha asked.

"Yeah." Helen nodded. "Josh needs one. Not me, though. My nostrils are naturally hairless because I have a condition called nostril-pecia."

Tabitha looked around, hoping someone would save her from this woman and her nostril stories. But Helen kept talking.

"You will not find one hair in this nose. On account of that nostril-pecia."

Tabitha had to come up with her own escape. "I'm going to go get some punch," she said desperately.

Helen watched her go, wondering why people always disappeared when she talked about her condition. It wasn't like she was contagious or anything.

Josh slammed into the kitchen and searched through the cabinets for something to eat, muttering to himself the whole time. Anger made him hungry. He poured a bowl of cereal and sat down at the table.

"Stupid Drake forgets my birthday," he grumbled. "Stupid Tabitha!" He poured milk into his cereal and took a spoonful. It was only after he started gagging that he checked the milk carton. He had grabbed his mom's soy milk by mistake. "Stupid soy milk!" he yelled.

As if that weren't bad enough, Megan's virtual pet was making a ton of noise in the living room. Couldn't he even eat a bowl of cereal in peace on his birthday?

Josh banged through the door, back into the living room. "Will you shut that dumb virtual pet up, please?"

Megan was totally frustrated herself. "Like I'm not trying?" she yelled back at him. "This thing won't let me sleep." Her words were punctuated by annoying high-pitched yips.

"Then yank out the batteries or just turn it off," Josh said.

"I can't. If I let Toby die, Janie will never talk to me again," Megan said.

"Well, maybe you'd be better off," Josh said, throwing his arms up into the air. Who needed friends, he thought. Who needed brothers? They only disappointed you in the end anyway.

"Huh?" Megan asked.

"Who needs people in their life, you know?"

Megan watched dumbfounded while Josh started to rant, pacing around the living room.

"They just hurt, okay?" he yelled. "They borrow your money without asking. They spill iced coffee all over your fresh underpants. And I'm, like, dude —"

Megan stood, cutting him off. Clearly Josh was totally upset with someone. "Okay, who set you off?" she asked.

"Drake, that's who," Josh spat. "He forgets my birthday, but then he throws a huge surprise birthday party for his fluffy new girlfriend who he's known for five days." He stared at the floor, totally upset. Did he mean so little to his brother?

Megan looked at him with her most sympathetic expression. "Look, I know how bad you must feel right now," she said. "But tomorrow morning, I guarantee you'll feel much worse."

Josh never knew what Megan would pull next, and that was scary — totally scary. "That doesn't make me feel any better," he said.

"I know," Megan said with a happy shrug. "'Night!"

She carried her virtual pet upstairs. It had just started to bark again. "Quiet, Toby!"

Josh watched her leave. He was still angry at Drake, only now his anger was joined by dread. What kind of evil plot did Megan have up her sleeve now?

CHAPTER FOUR

Josh was still trying to figure out how to protect himself from Megan's next prank when Drake ran in.

"Josh!"

"I'm not speaking to you," Josh said, heading back into the kitchen.

Drake followed him in. "Look, I'm sorry I forgot your birthday."

"Sorry doesn't treat my teeth," Josh yelled, still walking away from his brother.

Treat my teeth? What did that mean? "One more time?" Drake asked, staying on his brother's heels.

"Just don't talk to me," Josh said. He didn't even want to look at Drake's face. In fact, he was seriously considering moving out of the bedroom they shared and into the garage, or the basement, or the attic — anywhere he wouldn't have to look at Drake or listen to his stupid bongo drums.

"If you just let me show you something, I'm sure it will cheer you up," Drake said.

Josh was sure he had already seen it, and it didn't cheer him up. "I've seen the birthmark on your back, Drake," Josh snapped. "It does not look like a giraffe raking leaves."

"No, not that," Drake answered, although he was totally convinced his birthmark did look like a giraffe raking leaves. So was Trevor. But now he had something else in mind, and it would definitely cheer Josh up — way up.

Drake reached into his pocket and pulled out an envelope. "These," he said, handing the envelope to Josh.

Josh snatched it from him, convinced that it was just another one of Drake's lame attempts at an apology. "What is this, huh? What do you consider —" Then Josh got a look at what was inside.

"Whoaaaaaaaaa!" he screamed. "Whoaaaaaaaaa! Whoaaaaaaaaa! Whoaaaaaaaaa! You got me tickets to Oprah!"

Drake threw his arms out wide with a huge smile. "Hug me, brothah!"

Josh did more than hug. He lifted Drake into a big bear hug and swung him around before setting him back down. "How did you do this?" he asked, totally amazed. "Oprah's only going to be in San Diego for one day. These tickets are impossible to get."

"Well, you know the guy who plays bass in my band?" Drake asked.

"Julio?"

"Yeah. Julio's dad is a sound mixer down at Radcliff Studios where Oprah's going to be doing the show," Drake explained.

"Get out!" Josh looked at the tickets. He still couldn't believe that he was actually holding two tickets to the *Oprah* show in his hand. This was the best present he had ever gotten. There was no question as to who Josh would take to the show with him. It had to be Drake.

"Yeah, so I went down to Julio's house, talked to his dad, got the tickets. Oh —" Drake cut himself off and pretended to be nonchalant about what was coming next. He had almost forgotten the best part in all the excitement. He pulled two laminated cards out of his pocket with a flourish and held them in front of Josh. "And backstage passes."

Now Josh was really screaming. He grabbed the passes from Drake and stared at them like they were gold.

Neither brother noticed Megan steal into the room with a camera. She didn't know what all the fuss was about, but Josh was screaming like a little girl and that was always a good thing to capture on film.

"So, do you love me again?" Drake asked. He had pretended getting the tickets was a breeze, but he had had to jump through some pretty big hoops to get those tickets for Josh. If this didn't make Josh forgive him, nothing would.

"Love you?" Josh asked. He grabbed Drake's arm, pulled him into another hug, and laid a big wet kiss on his cheek.

Megan popped up just in time with her camera. "Okay," she laughed, checking the digital image. "This is sooooo going on the Internet."

Josh barely noticed. He was still totally and completely amazed. Not only was he going to see Oprah's show but he had actual backstage passes. He might even get to meet her!

Drake wiped his cheek in disgust. How did Megan always manage to capture his most embarrassing moments on film, he wondered?

The next day, Josh pulled his car into the Radcliff Studios parking lot. He was wearing a bright blue T-shirt with his favorite picture of Oprah on the front. Drake, who dressed the way he always did — in jeans and a vintage logo T-shirt — had tried to talk Josh into wearing something less geeky, but Josh was convinced the shirt would get Oprah to notice him. Maybe she'd even autograph her own face!

"Do you think I might actually get to speak to Oprah?" Josh asked, his voice high with excitement.

"Maybe." Drake looked out the window for a parking spot. The lot was pretty full.

"Oh ho!" Josh said with a huge smile. "I can't stand it!"

Drake thought that Josh was acting like a complete spaz. It was time to calm him down, or he'd totally embarrass them both. "All right. Chill out, dude, okay," Drake said. "Celebrities don't like it when people get all spazzy."

Drake noticed a parking spot and pointed. "Park there."

"No, I want to find a spot closer to the door," Josh answered.

"Why?" Drake asked. What was the difference where they parked? he wondered.

"Because, if we park far away, then I might have to walk too far and I could get sweaty," Josh reasoned. Meeting Oprah was the most important moment of his life so far, and it had to be perfect. "I will not meet Oprah with pit stains."

Drake looked at his brother as if he had totally lost his mind. They were passing up perfectly good parking spots because Josh had overactive sweat glands? "Just park the car already," he said impatiently. He reached over from the passenger seat and tried to turn the steering wheel in the direction of a parking space.

"Would you let go of my steering wheel?" Josh said, turning it in the other direction.

"No, would you just park!" Drake struggled to turn the wheel again.

"Hey, c'mon," Josh said, fighting back.

The brothers fought for control of the wheel, turning it one way, then another as they got closer to a group of autograph seekers and photographers in front of the studio. Josh tried to slam his foot on the brake, but it slipped off and hit the gas pedal. Suddenly the car bolted forward.

"Hey, watch it! Watch it!" Drake yelled.

Josh was watching, but his foot was stuck. He screamed as the car zoomed forward just as two women walked toward the studio with a security guard.

There was no time to stop. The guard was able to pull the first woman out of the way, but the second woman didn't have a chance.

Boom!

Josh's car and the woman collided with a sickening thump. Josh watched in horror as the woman rolled up the hood and onto his windshield. Then she rolled in the other direction and hit the sidewalk. It happened so fast there was nothing Josh could do.

"Oprah!" someone shrieked. "It's Oprah. Somebody call for help!"

Drake and Josh watched, shocked and terrified as the realization of what just happened sank in and the people around them ran for help.

"I ran over Oprah!" Josh screamed.

CHAPTER FIVE

Drake and Josh stood in the parking lot, watching the paramedics wheel Oprah's stretcher into an ambulance.

Josh was doing his best not to cry. "This is my worst birthday ever," he whimpered.

"Because you ran over Oprah?" Drake asked, totally calm.

Josh did a double take. Did Drake really just ask him that question? "No, because it's a little humid," he answered sarcastically. "Yes, because I ran over Oprah!"

Drake winced and stepped back.

Josh approached one of the paramedics. "Excuse me, sir, I was just wondering," he stammered. "Is Oprah going to be — you know — okay?" he asked with a hopeful expression.

"I'm afraid not, son," the paramedic said seriously.

Josh's face crumpled. His shoulders slumped. He

had killed Oprah. He was a murderer. "Oh no," Josh moaned.

The paramedic laughed. "I'm just messing with you," he said, patting Josh on the shoulder. "She'll be fine, just a couple of cuts and bruises."

Josh's jaw dropped. Did that guy really think Oprah's life — or death — was something to be joked about? Josh turned to his brother for comfort, but Drake was talking to another paramedic — a very pretty one.

"Here's my number," she said, handing Drake a slip of paper with a smile.

"Oh, thanks," Drake said, smiling back. "You'll definitely be the first person I call if I ever get into an accident."

Josh watched her walk away, then grabbed Drake's arm. "You're getting a girl's phone number when I just T-boned my favorite talk show host?"

"Hey, at least you got to meet her," Drake said. He obviously thought his brother was totally overreacting.

"No, no, no! The grille of my car got to meet

her, okay?" Josh cringed, remembering the moment — the awful *thunk*, followed by the sight of Oprah rolling onto his windshield and then hitting the ground. "Oh," he moaned. "I am going to be in so much trouble."

"Chill out, okay?" Drake said. "Her assistant said she's not going to press charges, so everything's fine."

"No. No. Okay? No. Everything is *not* fine," Josh insisted. "I can never watch Oprah again, because all I'm going to be able to do is think about how much she must hate me for almost killing her." Josh loved watching *Oprah*. He looked forward to it every day. And now she would be lost to him forever.

"Okay. Okay." Drake raised his hands in surrender and tried to calm his brother down with a soothing voice. "Look, this ambulance says Mercy Hospital."

But Josh wouldn't be soothed. "Yes. Yes. Yes," he snapped. "We all know you can read at a third-grade level. So?"

"So," Drake said slowly, deciding to ignore the

insult. "We go there, we find Oprah's room, and you apologize to her."

Josh thought about it for a minute. Could it be that simple? Could Drake's plan work? A smile slowly spread across his face. Oprah would forgive him and he could go back to being her number one fan. "Yeah. Yeah, that's good," Josh said, nodding.

"See, no worries." Drake started to walk to the front of the ambulance to say good-bye to the pretty paramedic. A woman with blond curly hair stopped him.

"Excuse me, are you the young man who ran over Oprah?" she asked with a smile.

"Oh no, that's my brother, Josh," Drake said helpfully.

The woman pointed and yelled at the group of women behind her. "He's the one."

Josh's happy fantasy of being forgiven by Oprah totally disappeared when he saw the angry mob of women running toward him. They were Oprah fans. They were mad. And they wanted revenge. The next

thing Josh knew, he was down on the ground screaming, "Ow! Ow! Ow!"

An hour later, Drake and Josh were walking
the halls of Mercy Hospital searching for Oprah's
room. They knew they had the right floor when
they saw a group of paparazzi clustered near the
nurses' station. How would Josh ever get past
them?

A guy in a suit was trying to move the press out of
the hospital. "All right. All right," he said. "All mem-
bers of the press are going to have to wait in the
hospital parking lot."

The photographers grumbled.

"We can't have you crowding the hallways," the
guy explained. "Please go."

The press grumbled some more, but they could tell
the hospital administrator meant business. He followed them to the elevator and got on with them to
make sure they left the building.

The only people left in the hall were two security
guards — one on either side of what had to be
Oprah's door.

"All right, now's our chance," Drake said to his brother. "Are you ready to meet Oprah?"

"How are we going to get past those goons?" Josh asked. The security guards looked a lot tougher and meaner than the ladies in the parking lot, and Josh hadn't been able to get past *them*. He rubbed a sore spot on his elbow.

But Drake had a secret weapon — his boyish charm. It worked on pretty girls, it worked on parents, and he was completely convinced that it would work on security guards. "Apparently you've forgotten," he said confidently. "I'm Drake."

Josh watched his brother swagger up to the first guard. "Hi, how're you doing?" Drake asked, running his hand through his shaggy brown hair.

The guard stared straight ahead. He didn't blink. He didn't move.

"We're just wondering if it's okay if my brother, Josh, and I go in and say a quick hello to Oprah," Drake said with a grin.

The guard didn't react.

"You know," Drake said, trying to lead him into a conversation. "Winfrey."

The guard still didn't blink.

Drake waved his hand in front of the guard's face. "Is that okay?" he asked.

There was still no response. It was like talking to a robot.

Was this guy even alive? Drake wondered. He shrugged. The guard didn't say no, so he'd take that as a yes. "Okay, c'mon," he said to Josh, reaching for the doorknob.

Now the guard moved. He reached out and zapped Drake in the arm with some kind of a stun gun.

Drake shook while the electric current moved through his body, then he slumped to the floor. He tried to stand, but his foot slipped out from under him. Slowly, holding on to the wall, he struggled to his feet. "Did you just stun me?" Drake asked, completely outraged.

The guard continued to stare straight ahead, as if Drake wasn't even there.

"All I did was ask if I could say hello to —"

The guard didn't answer. His facial expression didn't

change. He simply reached out and stunned Drake again, this time in the stomach.

Drake's jaw dropped. His eyes popped. His body quivered and shook. Then he slumped to the floor again.

Josh watched, totally stunned himself, while his brother slowly got to his feet again.

"Dude!" Drake yelled, looking into the face of his attacker. But the guard was stoic and silent.

Josh ran to his brother. "Drake, are you all right?"

"I don't know," Drake answered, checking to make sure all his limbs were still attached.

Josh turned to the second security guard. "If your friend over here has a problem with my brother, he should politely say to him —"

Josh's words were cut off by a Taser in his side. Like Drake, he quivered and shook and then crumpled onto the floor. He staggered to his feet, holding his head. "What was that for?" he asked the guard.

But like the first guard, this guy didn't answer. He didn't move. He didn't blink.

"Dude, are you okay?" Drake asked his brother.

"I don't know," Josh answered, echoing his brother's answer to the same question.

Drake was fuming. "This is *not* cool," he said to the first security guard. "All we want to do is say hello to Oprah."

He should have known what was coming by now, but Drake was totally surprised by the Taser to his shoulder. The next thing he knew, his head was swirling and he was on the floor again.

"You guys are just mean, okay?" Josh said. "And if Oprah knew that you guys were doing this —"

Josh joined his brother on the floor, right after he took a Taser in the gut.

Talking was obviously getting them nowhere. The brothers exchanged glances and edged away from Oprah's door before climbing to their feet on wobbly legs.

"We're gonna go," Drake said as soon as they were out of reach.

Josh bit back a moan and held his stomach as they walked to the elevator. "Wow, that really hurt."

"It's all right, man. I have another idea," Drake said.

Josh was ready to give up. Clearly, he wasn't meant to meet Oprah. His attempts had so far proved painful for both of them. "Maybe we should just go home," he said.

"No!" Drake was determined to complete his mission. "I told you I was going to get you in to meet Oprah, and now I'm going to."

"How are we going to get past all these people?" Josh asked, waving his arm in the direction of the guards.

Drake didn't answer. He launched into his idea. "Flesh-eating virus!" he yelled at the top of his lungs, pointing to Josh. "This kid has a flesh-eating virus."

People started to scream. Patients, nurses, doctors — they all started running. No one wanted to catch a flesh-eating virus. They were supercontagious and superdeadly.

"He's very, very contagious," Drake yelled.

The security guards eyed each other. No way were they sticking around for this. They forgot all about guarding Oprah. They took off, practically knocking each other over in their hurry to get away from Josh.

"Clear the area quickly," Drake yelled. "A flesh-eating virus!"

Josh had rapidly caught on to the idea. "Oh, my

flesh," he moaned, holding on to his face like the skin was about to slip off. "Oh, my flesh is being eaten. Ow!"

His words overlapped Drake's warnings. "Go quickly. Quickly," he urged.

The floor emptied in a matter of seconds.

"Oh, my flesh," Josh groaned, doubling over like he was in terrible pain. Then he realized they were alone. "Oh, that was nice," he said with a laugh.

"Uh-huh." Drake grinned. "Now I believe you have a date with Oprah."

Josh suddenly became nervous. He tugged on his T-shirt, making sure Oprah's face was wrinkle-free. She looked perfect, but what about him? "My hair," he said, patting his pockets. "Thank you," he breathed when he found a comb. He was about to run it through his dark wavy hair and head for Oprah's door.

He was stopped by a scream.

"That's him!" a nurse yelled, coming onto the floor with a doctor. "That's the boy with the flesh-eating virus."

A hazardous materials team, covered in uniforms that looked like space suits, ran toward Drake and Josh.

"The one with the big head?" the doctor asked.

"Yes," the nurse confirmed. She was practically hysterical, keeping her distance from the germs.

"Okay, it's not that big, first of all," Josh said.

The hazmat team came up behind him and pulled him onto a stretcher.

"Whoa, wait a minute," Josh yelled, kicking his legs. "I'm feeling much better."

The hazmat team held him down, breathing oxygen through their helmets so they wouldn't catch his deadly germs. They started to wheel Josh away.

"Drake, help!" Josh screamed, still kicking.

Drake assessed the situation. Ten hazmat guys versus him. The hazmat guys would definitely win. The only thing Drake could do was watch as Josh was wheeled away. A small siren on the back of the stretcher warned people to stay away.

"We've got to get that man into a chemical bath — stat!" the doctor said.

Drake looked around. Should he tell someone that Josh didn't really have a flesh-eating virus? But there was no one to tell. The floor was empty. Then he spotted something that totally took his mind off the situation at hand — Oprah's lunch on a tray, right outside her door.

"Hey, mashed potatoes!" he said, picking up the small container. He stirred them up and took a big bite. *Hospital food isn't nearly as bad as people say it is*, he thought.

CHAPTER SIX

Drake sat on the couch in his room, playing the bongo drums. He had wandered around the hospital for a while, looking for Josh. Then he gave up and came home. He was sure Josh would be okay.

He heard Megan scream and he jumped. His free bongo drums broke in half and fell to the floor. "My bongos," he said, picking them up and heading for the desk. He'd have to find something to put them together again.

Megan ran into the room carrying her electronic game. "Toby's dying," she said, waving it in the air.

"What? Your electronic pet thingie?" Drake asked, pulling a roll of duct tape out of a desk drawer.

"Yes. I fell asleep for, like, forty-five minutes and now he's dehydrated," Megan said.

Drake stared at her, turning the roll of silver tape around on his thumb.

Megan rolled her eyes. "You don't know what dehydrated means, do you?"

"No," Drake admitted.

"He's dying of thirst," Megan said.

Drake ripped a piece of tape off the roll. "What dies of thirst in forty-five minutes?"

Megan rolled her eyes again. "Apparently Toby."

But Drake was much more focused on taping his drums back together. He wasn't even trying to help her.

"Ah, you're useless," Megan snapped before turning her back on him. "C'mon, Toby," she pleaded with the mini computer. "Live! Live!"

Megan ran out of the room, so caught up in begging Toby to hang on that she didn't notice Josh. And had she noticed, she definitely would have taken a picture.

Josh wore a hospital gown. His face, arms, and legs were a sickening splotchy red color. His elbows and his knees wouldn't bend, and he walked like a zombie from a horror movie. He winced in pain with each step, but he could hardly get his mouth open to make a sound.

He marched up to Drake like a wooden soldier and glared at him.

Drake looked up from his drums. "Hey, man!" he said, all casually.

"Hey, man?" Josh sneered.

"Hey, man," Drake said slowly, totally confused.

"You left me at the hospital to be chemically bathed," Josh said, pointing at his bright red skin.

"Oh, yeah," Drake remembered. "How'd that go?"

Josh's eyes widened in astonishment. "Oh, actually it was quite soothing, especially the part where they . . ." he said sarcastically. "Oh, it was horrible," he yelled.

Drake shook his head. Was Josh blaming him? "Okay, what up with the 'tude?" Drake asked.

"Do you know what it's like to have an involuntary chemical bath?" Josh asked.

Drake guessed Josh didn't really expect an answer, so he didn't even try to answer. Somehow he thought Josh would be sure to fill him in on the details, whether he wanted to hear them or not. So instead of answering, he finished taping his drums together and carried them over to the couch.

"It stings," Josh said. *"Everywhere."*

"All right, look," Drake said. "I'll tell you what. I'm going to make it up to you, okay?"

Josh had had it with Drake trying to make things up to him. "No. Okay? No you're not," Josh said, remembering all the disasters that had happened to him when Drake was supposedly trying to be nice. "Because that's when the badness happens. The only time you ever try to do anything nice for me is after you've caused me some kind of physical damage or emotional distress."

Drake stared at his brother with a blank expression while Josh ranted.

"You are never going to make up anything to me ever again," Josh insisted, shaking his head. He headed out of the room. He didn't even want to share the planet with Drake, let alone the same room.

"Wait," Drake said softly.

Josh stopped and turned to his brother. He'd give him a chance to apologize. He owed him that much.

But Drake didn't apologize. "Do these sound okay to you?" he asked, launching into a Latin rhythm on the bongos.

Josh didn't say a word. He slowly moved in front of

Drake and slammed his own hands on top of the drums, silencing the tune. Then he ripped the bongos apart and dropped them on the coffee table before heading for the door.

Ignoring Josh's bad mood, Drake watched him leave. "Could you bring me the hot glue gun?" he asked, still thinking about his drums.

"Not really," Josh yelled, slamming the door behind him.

Josh was relieved that Drake was out of the house for most of the next day. He was also relieved that he wasn't scheduled to work at the Premiere. The last thing he needed was to watch all the kids hanging out in the café, remembering that Drake had thrown a surprise party there for Tabitha on *his* birthday.

But then he got an urgent text message from Helen telling him to get to the Premiere ASAP. Josh took his job seriously. If there was an emergency, Helen knew he would come to her rescue. At least she appreciated him, even if Drake didn't.

Josh ran into the theater totally out of breath from his race to get there. "Helen! I got here as fast as I could. Do you need me to unclog the butter hose?" Josh didn't like to brag, but he had a special touch with the butter hose.

"Josh, there's no clog in the butter hose," Helen answered.

"But you just text messaged me and said there was a huge clog —"

"*Surprise!*"

Josh turned around to find all his friends ready to celebrate his birthday. His jaw dropped. He was too stunned to scream. He couldn't believe it — a surprise party for him! The café was filled with blue and red balloons. Drake stood in the center of the crowd with a huge smile on his face.

"Happy Birthday, man," Drake said when Josh walked over.

"Drake, I can't believe you did this for me," Josh said. Then he remembered how embarrassed he was the last time he thought a party was for him. "This is for me, right?"

"Yes," Drake said. "And there's more." He reached

behind him for a piece of paper. "Mom and Dad got a call from Oprah's lawyer."

"Her lawyer?" Josh asked, suddenly worried. Was this also a "good-bye, you're going to jail for the rest of your life" party?

"Yeah, I guess she's kind of peeved that you ran her over," Drake said with a shrug. "Look what they sent to the house."

Josh took the paper from Drake and looked it over. "A restraining order?"

"Yeah, it says by law you can't get within three hundred feet of Oprah."

Josh didn't get it. Why was Drake giving this to him like it was a present? "And why is this happy news?" he asked sarcastically.

"Check the signature at the bottom," Drake said with a grin.

Josh checked out the restraining order again. He gasped. "Oprah Winfrey! She signed it!"

"Yup," Drake said.

Now Josh was ready to scream with excitement. "I got an autograph from Oprah!" he yelled, waving the paper above his head.

Everybody knew how much Josh loved Oprah. His friends cheered and clapped.

"Yeah!" Josh yelled, looking at the paper again.

Drake pulled his brother aside. "Look, man, I'm really sorry I forgot your birthday," he said quietly.

Josh shook his head. Having Drake as a brother could be totally maddening, but he knew Drake really cared about him — whether he remembered birthdays or not. "It's okay," Josh said.

"No it's not," Drake answered. "So I got you something special."

"Dude, you didn't have to."

"Just wait," Drake said, running out of the café.

Josh showed his Oprah autograph to Craig and Eric while he waited. "How cool is that?" he asked. "I think I'm going to put it over my bed," he said.

Craig's and Eric's attention was drawn away. Josh turned to see what they were looking at and he gasped again.

Drake had wheeled in a shiny silver motor scooter with a huge yellow bow. "Happy Birthday!" he said.

Now Josh really couldn't believe his eyes. "You got

me a Vespa?" he asked. "But, dude, how did you afford that?" Then he answered his own question. "Oh, Dad's credit card."

"Yeah," Drake said with a shrug. He'd be in trouble when Walter Nichols found out, but it was worth it for the thrilled expression on Josh's face.

"You're the best," Josh said.

"I know," Drake answered. He patted the Vespa's seat. "C'mon, hop on. See how she feels."

Josh didn't have to be asked twice. He handed his restraining order to Drake and threw one leg over the seat before turning the key. The Vespa roared to life. "This thing is awesome!" he said, feeling it shake underneath him. "But how do you —"

It was too late. The scooter had already taken off and Josh had no idea where the brake was. All he could do was steer and hope he didn't hit anything — again. Unfortunately, Helen had just left the concession stand with two big tubs of popcorn.

She screamed and jumped out of his way just in time, but the popcorn flew everywhere.

"Uh-oh." Drake snuck out of the Premiere. Drake

had heard Helen yell before, and he didn't want to have to live through the experience again. Then it hit him — he had gotten Josh into trouble *again*.

Maybe Josh was right, maybe he didn't have bad luck. He had Drake.

Josh would have been thinking the same thing, if he hadn't been so busy trying not to crash.

Part Two:
Vicious Tiberius

Prologue

Josh stood in the hallway at school struggling to get his locker open. The door was always getting stuck. "I'll tell you this," he said, pulling on the latch. "Handling a bad situation can be *very* stressful."

Drake lay on the couch in his room with his feet up on the coffee table and a bag of balloons — leftovers from Josh's surprise party — in his lap. "Watching Josh deal with a bad situation can be *very* hysterical." he said.

Josh tugged harder on the locker's handle. It wouldn't budge. But fighting with his locker wasn't the bad situation he was thinking of. "Like the time I donated blood," he said.

Drake blew up a yellow balloon. "Like the time he donated blood at school." he said, letting the balloon go. It flew around the room until it was completely out of air and landed on the floor.

Josh put his foot up against the locker and yanked on the handle even harder. It still wouldn't budge. "So this attractive nurse sticks a needle in my arm, right?"

"This insanely pretty nurse shoves a needle in Josh's arm." Drake said. The nurse was almost pretty enough to get Drake to volunteer to give his own blood. Then he remembered there were needles involved.

Josh pulled his emergency screwdriver out of his backpack. He slipped it behind the door and used it like a lever. The locker flew open, almost hitting him in the face. "But no one told me that it was the nurse's first day on the job."

Drake played with a purple balloon. "It was her first day being a nurse." he said. chuckling.

Josh got mad all over again, remembering. "So as soon as my blood starts coming out..."

Drake cracked up. remembering. "When she sees the first drop of Josh's blood..."

"She faints!" Josh explained.

"She passes out!" Drake laughed.

"And when she fell down, the tube slipped off the needle and my blood started spurting all over the room." Josh still couldn't believe it. "*Spurting!*" he repeated, using his arm to demonstrate.

"Josh's tube was spewing blood like a garden hose." Drake said.

Josh hadn't thought it could get any worse. But it had. "Oh yeah, after I lose, like, a quart of blood, I pass out."

Drake didn't think it could get any funnier. But it had. "Then he fainted," he said with a laugh.

"I was soooo unconscious," Josh said, getting outraged all over again. "I got blood all over my blue sweater."

Drake cracked up again. "Yeah, good times."

Josh reached into his locker and pulled out the sweater. It was covered in dark red splotches. He was in a total frenzy now. "Look at this sweater," he demanded. "Look at it!"

CHAPTER ONE

Drake and Josh were both in Mrs. Hayfer's English class. Josh listened attentively to the lecture about *Tom Sawyer* and *Huckleberry Finn*. Drake stared out the window.

"You know, another interesting piece of trivia about Mark Twain is that before he was an author he worked for a company that manufactured chewing gum," Mrs. Hayfer said, walking around to the front of her desk. "So I guess you could call him a chew chew Twain." Mrs. Hayfer laughed.

The class simply stared at her. Why was she laughing? they wondered. Was that supposed to be funny?

"Why don't you people ever laugh at my jokes?" Mrs. Hayfer asked, totally frustrated.

The bell rang, and the class was saved from a long speech about why Mrs. Hayfer thought her jokes were funny. At least for today.

"Okay, don't forget to hand in your essays before you leave," she said.

Most of the class simply dropped their essays onto the desk, but Josh made sure to put his directly into Mrs. Hayfer's hands. Drake called it sucking up. Josh called it smart. "Here's my essay, Mrs. Hayfer," he said proudly.

"Oh, how nice," Mrs. Hayfer said, taking his carefully bound essay. "I'm a sucker for translucent lavender," she said, admiring the binder.

"Well, who isn't?" Josh said with a smile.

Drake dropped his assignment on Mrs. Hayfer's desk and tried to sneak out unnoticed. But he wasn't fast enough.

"Drake," Mrs. Hayfer said.

"Yes, ma'am?"

"You were supposed to hand in an essay on current events." She held his assignment between the tips of her fingers like it had a contagious disease.

"Which I did," Drake said with a cocky smile.

"No," Mrs. Hayfer said firmly. She turned his "essay" around. It was a copy of the *San Diego Times*. "This is a copy of today's newspaper with your name written on top — in crayon."

"Well, you can't get more current than today's

paper, right, Josh?" Drake asked, calling on his brother for support.

Josh closed his eyes with a pained expression. He didn't want to get caught up in another disagreement between Mrs. Hayfer and his brother. Once he had been forced to represent Drake against Mrs. Hayfer in student court. Drake almost got expelled, and Josh right along with him. Then there was the time he and Drake had gotten into a huge fight over Sammy — the boy Mrs. Hayfer assigned to Drake in the Little Sibling program — no, Josh didn't need this.

"Please don't get me involved in this," Josh said. But he couldn't leave Drake alone with Mrs. Hayfer. He didn't even really know why, he just knew it was a bad idea — a *really* bad idea.

"You know what this means, Drake," Mrs. Hayfer said, dropping the newspaper on her desk.

Drake nodded. He had originally thought his newspaper idea was brilliant, but now he realized he should have known Hayfer would hate it. She wasn't exactly big on originality. And she actually thought he should waste his valuable free time on homework. "An F," he said.

"That is one question you always get right," Mrs. Hayfer said with a fake smile. "And guess what else?"

"What?" Drake asked grimly.

She dropped the fake smile. "I hate you."

"I know," Drake answered. It wasn't like she didn't tell him all the time.

Her cell phone rang and the brothers started to leave the room. "Stay!" Mrs. Hayfer ordered. Clearly she wasn't finished with them.

"Hello? Yes, Marta, what is it?" Mrs. Hayfer said into the phone. "Oh, I see." She held a finger up to Drake and Josh, keeping them in the room. "No, I'm not angry, it's fine," she said.

Clearly the person on the other end of the phone wasn't convinced by Mrs. Hayfer's tone of voice.

"I said I'm not angry," she yelled. "Good-bye!" Mrs. Hayfer closed her phone with an angry snap.

Drake winced. *She was probably imagining my head was caught between the two halves of her phone,* he thought.

Josh was concerned. "Is everything okay?" he asked.

"My housekeeper just canceled for the weekend. I'm going away and now I have no one to watch my house," Mrs. Hayfer explained.

Josh's face brightened. "Really?" he asked.

Drake knew what his brother was thinking. "Don't do it," he warned under his breath.

But Josh loved to help people. "I'll do it!" he volunteered.

"So he does it," Drake said to himself, crossing his arms. He had a feeling he'd get dragged into this, too, and there was no way he wanted to help Mrs. Hayfer with anything, except maybe a move out of state. The woman hated him.

"Josh, that's very sweet," Mrs. Hayfer said. "But I have a dog and lots of plants. You don't want to do all that."

"I'm great with dogs and plants," Josh said proudly. "Once, when I was little, I had a poodle and a fern. I named them both Jerry."

Drake stared at him. How did he end up with such a geeky brother? "Of course you did," he muttered sarcastically.

Josh waited for Mrs. Hayfer to say yes.

"Well, I really am stuck," she said slowly. "If you're sure you don't mind."

"No. I'm all over it," Josh assured her.

"Well, thank you, Josh." She smiled at him sweetly, and then turned to Drake with a much different expression. "And as for you, Drake," she said. "I spent five years in postgraduate school to become a teacher. I've won three national teaching awards. I'd appreciate it if you would show me and my assignments some respect."

Drake didn't hear any of her speech. He was too distracted by something on her face. He leaned in to get a closer look. "You know, you've got a little booger right there," he said, pointing to her nostril. "If you want to get it —"

Mrs. Hayfer totally lost it. She screamed something unintelligible and lunged at Drake, ready to strangle him.

Josh held her back. "He's not worth it," he told her.

She struggled some more, but Josh wouldn't let go.

"He's not worth it," Josh said again.

Drake ran out of the room.

CHAPTER TWO

Saturday afternoon, Drake and Josh wandered into the living room just in time to find their father, Walter Nichols, giving instructions to two deliverymen. They were setting up a high-tech elliptical exercise machine in the middle of the living room.

"All right, could you move it a little to the left?" Walter instructed.

"Oh, hey, Pop," Josh said.

"What's that thing?" Drake asked.

"Oh, it's an elliptical machine," Mr. Nichols answered.

Drake and Josh exchanged confused looks. What did their father want with an exercise machine, and what was it doing smack in the middle of the living room?

"Well, for who?" Josh asked.

"For me," Mr. Nichols answered. "I'm going to start working out."

Drake and Josh cracked up. The idea of their dad working out was just too hilarious.

"Okay, okay," Mr. Nichols said, obviously offended. "I'd like to know what's so funny about me working out."

"Oh, nothing." Drake tried to stop laughing. He couldn't. "You see . . . it's just the thought of you actually, uh, working out."

Josh cracked up again.

Walter sighed. "I bought it because I'm competing in Channel Seven's Annual Five-K Fun Run," he told them.

"Again?" Drake asked. "But doesn't that other weatherman always beat you? What's his name?"

"Bruce Winchell," Josh said.

"I told you never to mention his name in this house," Mr. Nichols said, totally annoyed. Not only had Bruce Winchell won the Fun Run five years in a row, he also kept winning the award for San Diego's Best Weatherman. "And for the record, I'm going to win this year."

Drake thought that could only mean one thing. "Bruce Winchell's not running?"

Now Mr. Nichols was really offended. "He's running. I'm just going to run faster."

Even the delivery guys cracked up at the idea of Mr. Nichols running faster than anyone. He shot them an angry look and they got serious again, tightening the bolts on the elliptical machine.

"I'm going to grab a Mocha Cola," Drake said to Josh.

"Hey, car keys," Josh reminded him.

Drake threw him the keys.

"Where are you headed?" Mr. Nichols asked.

"Oh, I promised my teacher that I would take care of her house while she's out of town," Josh said. "So I'm just going to feed her dog and water her plants and stuff."

"Oh, good. On the way home, would you pick Megan up from oboe practice?" Mr. Nichols asked. "I'm going to be here all night working out."

They heard Drake laughing all the way from the kitchen.

"It's not funny," Mr. Nichols yelled.

"I'll pick up Megan," Josh said, trying not to laugh too hard.

"Thank you," Mr. Nichols said.

"See you in an hour."

Drake met his brother at the door. "Hey, I'm going to ride with you."

"Why?" Josh asked.

"Well, because I want to help you do stuff for Mrs. Hayfer."

Josh didn't have to say "I don't believe you —" the look on his face said it for him.

"Okay," Drake admitted. "The cheerleaders practice outside on Saturdays and it's on the way. So, let's drive by — slowly."

"No," Josh said, heading for the door. "We're not going to gawk at cheerleaders."

Drake put out his hand to stop him. "Lori McNeill and Karen Franklin are going to be there," he said in a singsong voice.

"They will?" Josh asked.

"Yes they will," Drake answered. He knew Josh had secret crushes on both girls.

"And you're sure they're going to practice outside?"

"If we're lucky," Drake said, still singing.

Josh thought about it for a second. "We'll drive by the cheerleaders," he agreed.

A little while later, Josh let himself into Mrs. Hayfer's house. Drake was right behind him.

"Why is it so much fun to watch cheerleaders?" Josh asked.

"Don't question it — just love it," Drake answered.

"True that." Josh looked around. He didn't know what he expected a teacher's house to look like — maybe something dark and dusty and full of books. But Mrs. Hayfer's house was light and airy and full of plants. "Hey, Mrs. Hayfer has a pretty nice place."

"I've seen nicer," Drake said, heading over to an entertainment center.

"All right, she said she'd leave me a note. . . ." Josh checked the end tables. "Which should be right . . ." He spotted it on the coffee table. "Here."

Josh read the note to himself, then spotted Drake poking around in Mrs. Hayfer's things. "Hey, hey, hey. No snooping."

"I'm not snooping," Drake said. "I'm rifling through her drawers to see what lies within."

"Well, I'm in charge," Josh told him. "And I don't want you rifling through Mrs. Hayfer's drawers."

Drake started to giggle.

"Oh, grow up!" Josh said.

Drake spotted a framed photograph of a blond girl in a beauty pageant gown and tiara. "Wow. This girl is seriously pretty," he said, reading the label on the picture. "Miss New Jersey, 1976."

Josh checked out the photo. "That's Mrs. Hayfer," he said.

Drake did a double take. "That's Mrs. Hayfer?" Then another question came to him. "There's a *new* Jersey?" English wasn't the only class that bored him. Add geography to the list. It was much more fun to stare out the window than to listen to the teacher.

Josh rolled his eyes. "Yeah, they just opened it," he said sarcastically. He snatched the picture from Drake and put it back on the shelf. "Now just stay put while I water the plants."

Josh grabbed the watering can and took care of the plants in the living room.

Drake opened the drawer again and started looking through Mrs. Hayfer's DVDs. He pulled one out and read it out loud. "'*Search for the Stars*'?"

"Will you put that back?" Josh said, looking up from an African violet.

"I want to see what it is," Drake said.

Josh realized that if Drake watched a DVD he would at least stay out of the rest of Mrs. Hayfer's other things. "All right. Fine," he snapped. "Just make sure you leave everything the way it was."

"Yeah, yeah, yeah," Drake said, waving his palm in Josh's direction so he would be sure to know Drake was listening. "Noise, noise."

Drake put the disc in the DVD player and hit PLAY. A much younger Mrs. Hayfer appeared on the TV screen.

"So, how about those turnpikes?" she asked.

Drake's jaw dropped. His eyes popped. "No way," he said. Mrs. Hayfer was on stage doing a comedy routine!

"What is it?" Josh asked from across the room

"It's Mrs. Hayfer on *Search for the Stars*! From like — from a million years ago!" he said.

"Get out of here!" Josh said. He couldn't believe it, either.

"Yeah! She's doing stand-up comedy."

Josh ran over. The brothers both stared at the TV in awe, watching a much younger Mrs. Hayfer totally bomb onstage.

"So who here is from New Jersey?" she asked the crowd.

No one answered.

"Well, we've got a diner there and there's this really old waitress and she has a name tag that said Ethel Lincoln, and I said, 'Oh, are you a descendant of Abraham Lincoln's?' And she said, 'Descendant? I'm his mother!' Am I right?"

Mrs. Hayfer paused for a laugh. There wasn't one.

Josh chuckled out of sympathy.

Drake shot him a look.

"It wasn't funny," Josh agreed.

The brothers kept watching, but it was getting even worse. Mrs. Hayfer knew her jokes were totally bombing, but she tried to keep going.

"Well, so . . . I have a cat," she said finally.

There was a crashing sound on the DVD.

"Okay," Mrs. Hayfer said, narrowing her eyes at the audience. Now she was acting like the Mrs. Hayfer Drake knew. "Who threw the chair?" she demanded.

Drake leaned in closer to the TV and pointed. There was something else that reminded him of the English teacher Mrs. Hayfer was today — the one who did her best to ruin his life. "Hey, she's got a booger in her nose there, too."

A Rottweiller ran into the room, sat on the floor, and barked.

Drake turned away from the TV. "Oh, look. A dog."

"Oh yeah. His name is . . ." Josh checked the list Mrs. Hayfer left for him. "Tiberius. I'm supposed to feed him and give him his ear medicine. Which is . . ." He looked around the room and spotted a bottle on the coffee table. "Right here. Will you hold his ear while I put the drops in?" Josh asked.

Drake stepped back, his face screwed up in disgust. "I don't want to touch a dog's infected ear. Gross!"

Josh looked at his brother like he was crazy. Since when did Drake find anything too gross to touch? "Gross?" he asked. "On the way here you ate a peanut off the car floor."

"It was honey roasted," Drake said in his own defense.

"Hold the ear!" Josh ordered.

"Fine," Drake muttered. He moved toward the dog.

Josh took the cap off the medicine. "Hi, Tiberius," he said in a high-pitched voice, moving toward the dog. "This is my brother, Drake, and he's going to hold your ear while I —"

Drake reached for Tiberius's ear. The dog bristled and then went completely crazy. He got to his feet and started barking viciously. Then the next thing the brothers knew, they were running for their lives. Tiberius was chasing them around the living room — growling, barking, and snapping his enormous teeth.

Drake and Josh screamed. They raced around the sofa and went through the first door they saw. Tiberius was right on their heels. They slammed the door to

Mrs. Hayfer's powder room just a half a second before Tiberius could sink his teeth into them.

Tiberius barked and scratched at the door, determined to get at them.

The only thing standing between the guys and sure death was a thin wooden door.

CHAPTER THREE

Josh was completely out of breath. He leaned against the door, trying to keep it closed against the crazed dog. Tiberius barked ferociously and pushed against the door, fighting to get in. Panting, Drake finally managed to lock it.

"Did you see those teeth?" Drake asked.

"Do you see this stain?" Josh said, pointing to his pants.

Drake took that as a yes.

Tiberius clawed at the closed door, determined to get to the guys. He threw himself against it, and the whole door shook.

The brothers cowered on the other side, totally terrified that Tiberius would break through.

Josh had never seen a dog so vicious, or so scary. "Man, what is that dog's problem?" he asked.

"Its problem is, it wants to eat us and we're in here!" Drake said.

Tiberius barked even harder when he heard the guys' voices.

"Mrs. Hayfer asks you to watch her house, but she doesn't mention that her dog is homicidal?" Drake asked sarcastically. It crossed his mind that maybe Mrs. Hayfer really wanted him dead, and had used Josh to put her least favorite student within range of her dog's huge teeth.

Josh checked the note Mrs. Hayfer had left for him. "It's not on the list!"

Suddenly, the barking stopped. They couldn't even hear the dog breathing.

"It stopped," Josh whispered.

"Yeah," Drake said, straining to hear something.

"Maybe he went into another room," Josh said. "Go outside and check."

Drake looked at his brother like he had totally lost his mind. "You check," he said, pushing Josh in front of him.

"No. I'm scared." Josh's whole body trembled.

"Oh, and I'm in here because I love hanging with you by a toilet?" Drake asked.

"C'mon," Josh said, pushing his brother toward the door.

Drake gave in. One of them had to check, and Josh probably looked more delicious to a dog. "All right," he said reluctantly.

He unlocked the door and slowly put his hand on the knob. But he couldn't bring himself to open the door.

"You just turn it," Josh said impatiently.

"I know," Drake snapped. He opened the door slightly and peered through the crack, ready to slam it again at the first sign of sharp teeth.

"Do you see him?" Josh asked.

"No. I think he's gone. Okay, now let's just walk out slowly —"

But that's exactly what Tiberius was waiting for. Suddenly he shoved his whole face through the door's opening, barking viciously. Drake and Josh desperately pushed against the door, trying to keep the dog out of the bathroom. Finally, they got the door closed and locked while Tiberius clawed and scratched on the other side.

The guys stared at each other in horror as they slid

to the floor, panicked and exhausted. "Oh my gosh!" they said in unison.

"How are we going to get out of here?" Drake asked. He looked around the room — there was no window, no way out.

"We've got to get help," Josh realized. He pulled out his cell phone. "I'll call Dad."

"Oh, great," Drake said sarcastically. What could their dad do, offer himself up as a human sacrifice?

Josh just stared at him. Drake really didn't give Josh's dad enough credit.

Drake changed his tune for Josh's benefit. "Oh, great!" he said again, pretending to be enthusiastic.

Josh dialed. What he didn't know was that Walter was working out hard on his new exercise machine. Someone had told him that music made exercise go faster, so he had pumped up the volume on his portable music player and sang along to one of Drake's songs.

> *"I'm on a highway to nowhere,*
> *tryin' to get by without you.*
> *I don't know why it took me so long to . . ."*

Between the music and the earphones, Mr. Nichols didn't hear a thing.

Josh listened to the phone ring on the other end.

"Well?" Drake asked.

"No answer," Josh told him.

Drake shook his head. That didn't make sense. Mr. Nichols was supposed to be home, working out, all afternoon. "You probably dialed the wrong number," Drake said, reaching for the phone. "Let me see it."

Josh wouldn't let go. It was his phone. "I think I know our own number," he said.

Drake tugged on the cell phone. "Dude, let me just try to —"

The guys fought for the phone. Drake wanted it, and Josh refused to give it up. Then it popped out of both of their hands and landed right in Mrs. Hayfer's toilet with a loud plop.

They walked over and peered into the toilet. The phone sat at the bottom.

"Niiiiice," Drake drawled.

"It's your fault," Josh snapped. "Go get it."

"No! I'm not putting my hand in here. That's Mrs. Hayfer's toilet," Drake said.

Josh peered in again. "Ah, it probably doesn't even work anymore," he said.

"Yeah, well, let's see." Drake hit the handle.

The toilet flushed.

Josh watched the cell phone circle in the water and then go down the drain, along with their chance to escape.

"It still works," Drake said brightly.

Josh closed his eyes in disgust. Drake had just sent his phone into the sewer system. Now they were really trapped. Josh tried not to yell. "I knew the toilet still worked, Drake," he said between clenched teeth. "I meant my phone."

"Oh," Drake answered. "Well, that's gone."

"Give me your phone," Josh said.

Drake patted his pockets. They were empty.

"Now what?" Josh asked.

He pointed to the living room and Tiberius. "I set it down out there, when I put the DVD in."

"*Niiiiice,*" Josh said, imitating his brother.

"Well, look," Drake reasoned. "The dog hasn't barked for a while, so he's probably in another room."

"So?" Josh asked.

"So, run out there, grab my phone, and come back before Tiberius kills you."

Josh didn't think that was such a good plan. Besides, he wasn't the one who left his phone lying around. "You're faster than me," he said. "So it's less dangerous if you go."

"Okay, fine," Drake said. How did he get stuck with this job when Josh was the one who had agreed to watch the homicidal dog in the first place? He'd have to be super fast. "Open the door on three," he said.

"Okay." Josh held the doorknob, ready to turn.

Drake crouched, ready to run. "Okay. One . . . two . . . three!"

Drake ran for the door at full speed, but instead of racing into the living room he hit the door and dropped to the floor with a thud. He rolled over, rubbing his forehead while Josh checked the door for damage.

Drake slowly got to his feet and shot an angry look at this brother.

"You hit the door," Josh said, stating the obvious.

"Yeah, why didn't you open it?" Drake asked, his voice tight with rage.

"You didn't say go," Josh answered.

"I said on three!" Drake insisted.

"Yeah," Josh agreed, counting on his fingers. "One, two, three . . . go!"

Drake threw his arms up in the air. Where did Josh get this stuff? "Fine! On go." He crouched down into a sprinter's stance again. "One . . . two . . . three . . . GO!"

Josh opened the door. Drake sprinted into the living room at full speed. He hurdled over the couch and grabbed his cell phone, holding it over his head in triumph. "I got it!" he yelled.

It was only when he turned around that he saw Tiberius lying on the couch, waiting for him.

Tiberius got to his feet. A low growl rose from deep in his throat.

Drake froze. He was practically face-to-face with a vicious animal that only wanted to rip him to shreds. "Hi there, Tiberius," he said in the calmest voice he could muster. "Lie down?" he asked. But Tiberius didn't lie down. He growled again. "No, okay, um . . ." Drake racked his brain for a command that Tiberius might follow.

Tiberius had other ideas. The dog went berserk again, barking at the top of his lungs, growling, and snapping his sharp teeth.

Terrified, Drake threw his cell phone into the air and ran. Tiberius snapped at his heels. Drake jumped on the couch and then over it before slamming into the powder room, knocking Josh in the head with the door. He managed to get the door closed and locked just before Tiberius could sink his teeth into him.

"Head trauma," Josh said, holding his head and staggering around the bathroom. "What happened?"

Drake was totally freaked. "Tiberius tried to snack on my face, that's what happened!"

"Did you get the cell phone?" Josh asked.

"Yeah," Drake answered in a small voice, not wanting to tell the full story.

"Yes!" Josh pumped his fist in the air.

"But I dropped it," Drake admitted.

"Aw, man!"

Slowly, the guys opened the door a crack and peeked out. Tiberius was on the floor, eating Drake's cell phone. After a few unsatisfying crunches, the dog spat out the phone in pieces. They realized that that's exactly what Tiberius wanted to do to them.

"You were so scared you couldn't hold on to the cell phone?" Josh asked.

"You wet your pants," Drake said in his own defense.

"This is true," Josh said.

Totally defeated, the brothers closed the door. Tiberius had won. They had no way out.

CHAPTER FOUR

Drake and Josh were still trapped in the powder room, so Drake decided to look through Mrs. Hayfer's medicine cabinet.

Josh slumped against the door. Now that both their cell phones were destroyed, he was totally out of ideas for rescue. Would they be stuck in here all weekend? "You realize we've been stuck in here for over an hour, don't you?" he asked.

"Yes, and don't whine to me," Drake answered. "You're the one who just had to go sucking up to Mrs. Hayfer." He imitated Josh, mocking him. "Oh, I'm-a-Josh, and I'd just love to take-a care of your house, Mrs. Hayfer."

Josh stared at his brother incredulously. Where'd that accent come from? "Okay, so when did I, like, become Italian?"

"You get my point."

"You think I want to spend my Saturday night

locked in my English teacher's bathroom with you?" Josh asked.

"Oh, c'mon, this is probably the most exciting Saturday night you've had in five years," Drake answered.

"Oh, you know what you . . ." Josh tried to come up with a snappy, insulting answer, but he couldn't. Drake was right. His Saturday nights weren't exactly the most exciting in town. "So?" he asked.

Drake sighed and went back to the medicine cabinet. So far he just found the usual — toothpaste, aspirin, Band-Aids. He was looking for dirt to use against Mrs. Hayfer.

"You know, you really shouldn't be looking through Mrs. Hayfer's medicine cabinet," he said.

Drake didn't stop. "Yeah, yeah," he muttered. "There's lots of stuff I shouldn't do." He pulled out a tube of medication and read the back. "Topical ointment. Apply twice daily to relieve itching." He stopped, totally disgusted, and threw the tube back into the cabinet, slamming the door. "Ewwww."

The brothers heard a voice calling to them from the living room. "Hello? Anybody home?"

"Who is that?" Josh whispered.

"It sounds like Megan," Drake whispered back.

Whoever it was called out again. "Drake? Josh?"

"That is Megan," Josh said. "How'd she get —" Suddenly he realized. "Oh no! She's outside with Tiberius!"

"He'll eat her alive!" Drake said.

"C'mon!"

Josh opened the door, but Drake immediately kicked it shut.

"Dude!" Josh yelled.

Drake threw himself in front of the door. Megan wouldn't risk her life for her brothers, so why should he risk his to save her? "Well! Just because she gets eaten doesn't mean we have to," he reasoned.

"That's our little sister out there," Josh argued. "And we've got to help her."

Drake shook his head. He knew Josh was right, as much as he hated to admit it. "All right," he said.

"C'mon," Josh said again.

The guys braced themselves and opened the door,

ready to run if they had to. They saw Megan sitting on the couch, petting Tiberius.

"Megan!" Josh said in a loud whisper, waving toward the front door. "Run!"

Megan laughed. "I don't want to run."

"But . . . he's vicious," Drake whispered, holding his hands up on either side of his face like claws.

Megan rolled her eyes and ruffled Tiberius's fur. "Yeah, he's real vicious."

Tiberius licked her check.

"Ooooh, down, boy," Megan joked. "You're so scary."

Drake and Josh couldn't believe it. They walked over to the couch and faced Megan. Tiberius was like a totally different dog. He was actually snuggling with their sister.

"I don't get it," Josh said. "He's all calm."

Drake thought about it for a minute, and then he understood. "Evil dog. Evil girl. Makes perfect sense."

Megan stood and walked toward the front door. Tiberius followed her calmly. "Where have you two been?" she asked, ignoring Drake's remark. "You were supposed to pick me up two hours ago."

"How'd you know we were here?" Josh asked.

"Dad said you were stopping here and then picking me up," she said. "Which you didn't."

"We couldn't," Josh said.

"Yeah, we were trapped here by this demon dog," Drake explained.

Megan looked at them like they were crazy. Tiberius sat calmly at her side. "What are you talking about?"

"When you're not around, he goes all berserk and tries to kill us," Josh said.

"Really?" Megan asked.

"Yeah," Josh said.

"Uh-huh," Drake agreed.

Megan thought about that for a second. Life would certainly be a lot easier without her annoying brothers. Besides, she didn't really believe Tiberius was a killer. He was just playing with her brothers, kind of like she did when she put hot sauce in their food or itching powder in their pajamas. It was all in fun.

"See ya!" Megan said happily, heading for the front door. She slammed it behind her.

Once again, Drake and Josh were alone with

Tiberius, and the dog stood between them and the front door. Tiberius started to bark the minute Megan was out of the house. The guys backed up slowly, trying to stay calm so that Tiberius wouldn't go berserk again. But the dog lunged at them, ready to bite.

Drake and Josh screamed and ran for their lives, making it into the safety of the powder room and slamming the door a half second ahead of the dog. They leaned against the door, while Tiberius once again barked and scratched on the other side.

CHAPTER FIVE

An hour later, Josh jumped from foot to foot, doing a weird jiggle dance. Finally, Drake couldn't take it anymore.

"Dude, you've been doing that for a half hour already. If you have to go, go!"

Josh stopped jiggling. His cheeks flushed. "I . . . I can't . . . not with you in here," he admitted.

"Why not?"

Josh stared at the floor. "I just can't."

Drake rolled his eyes. "Just think about waterfalls," he said.

"All right. Close your eyes," Josh told him, but then he forgot all about having to go to the bathroom.

"Hello," they heard a male voice call. "Anyone home?"

"Now who's here?" Drake asked.

"Hello?" the voice called again. "Animal Control."

"Animal Control!" Josh repeated. They were saved!

The guys slowly opened the door and peered out. Tiberius was nowhere to be seen, but a big guy with a pole stood by the front door.

"Hey," Drake said.

"Hi," Josh added.

"You guys have a canine issue?" the man asked.

"Yeah," Drake answered. "How did you know?"

"We got a call from one of the neighbors," he said, reading from a notepad. "Said she had heard loud barking and girls screaming all night long." The man, whose uniform indicated his name was Stan, looked around for girls. There weren't any — just Drake and Josh. "Are you the screaming girls?"

Drake and Josh didn't exactly want to answer that question. Drake's embarrassed "maybe" overlapped with Josh's mortified "sort of."

"Okay," Stan said. "Where's the dog?"

The brothers looked around again. They had been standing here for a whole minute, and they were still alive. Where was Tiberius?

"We're not sure," Drake told him.

"But you should put on some protective padding or something," Josh said.

"Yeah, this dog's big and way out of control," Drake explained.

Stan chuckled. "Look, boys, I've been doing this for eleven years. Don't worry about me. I can handle any dog situation that can possibly —"

Tiberius took that moment to make his presence known. He burst in from the kitchen with a ferocious bark, running toward the three guys at full speed. He got close enough for them to practically count his razor-sharp teeth.

Now Stan was the one who was screaming like a little girl. "Oh no!" he yelled, taking off in the direction of the powder room. He threw his pole into Josh's hands and pushed the guys out of his way.

Drake and Josh watched Stan dash into the bathroom, letting out a series of high-pitched screams in response to every single one of Tiberius's barks.

Terrified, Drake and Josh took off after him. Josh reached the door first. Stan went flying when Josh pushed the door open. But Josh still had the pole in his hands and he blocked his own entrance to the bathroom. He banged his Adam's apple on the pole and fell back into Drake's arms.

Tiberius was at Drake's heels, ready to take a big bite out of his leg. Drake managed to push Josh through the door and run in behind him. They slammed the door closed, listening to Tiberius bark and claw on the other side.

The Animal Control expert was cowering in the corner. They were trapped — again.

An hour later, Stan sat on the lid of the toilet while Drake and Josh slumped in opposite corners of the small powder room.

"So, you've been an Animal Control guy for eleven years, huh?" Drake asked sarcastically.

"Trained to handle any kind of dog situation, have you?" Josh added.

"I've never seen a dog like this one," Stan said. "I've never seen anything this scary. And I fought in 'Nam."

"'Nam?" Drake asked.

Stan rolled his eyes. "You know — Vietnam."

Drake thought about that for a minute. He sort of

remembered hearing about a Vietnam. "Where's that?" he asked. "New Jersey?"

Stan turned to Josh. "What's wrong with him?" he asked, cocking his head in Drake's direction.

Josh shook his head. He knew exactly where Vietnam was, but then again, he paid attention in class. That was something Drake never did. "Yeah, we're not sure."

Drake jumped to his feet. "Look, do you want to spend the rest of our Saturday night insulting me?" he asked his brother. "Or do you want to figure a way out of here?"

Josh wanted out. He was totally frustrated. Help had finally arrived and they were still stuck. "I mean, you're the Animal Control guy," he said to Stan. "Why don't you go out there and control that beast?"

Stan shook his head. "Nooooo. I'm not going out there and let that monster chew my arm off. I'm going to sit right here on this toilet. Thank you very much."

"Well, fine," Josh said. He pointed to himself and Drake. "We're getting out of here — right now."

"Good luck, hamburger meat," Stan answered.

Drake was leaning against the sink.

"Hey, hand me that bar of soap over there," Stan said.

Drake handed Stan the soap with an annoyed expression, and got even madder when Stan took out a small knife and started carving.

"What?" Stan asked, feeling their eyes on him. "You've never seen a man whittling on a toilet?"

"Actually, no," Drake said.

"No we haven't," Josh confirmed.

They both turned away from Stan. Clearly he was settling in for the long haul.

"All right," Drake said to Josh. "So how do we get out of here?"

"Well, I think if we run out and split up — just run in different directions — we'll confuse him and we'll get to the door before he can kill us," Josh said thoughtfully. "You want to go for it?"

Suddenly the powder room was looking pretty cozy. "I don't know," Drake said. "It's kind of risky."

"Hey, young man," Stan said, rubbing his shoulder.

"Feel this lump on my shoulder. You tell me if this should be removed."

Drake stared at Stan for a minute and weighed which was worse — feeling Stan's lump or risking his life with Tiberius. He turned to Josh. "Let's do it."

"On three," Josh said. "Ready?"

Drake nodded. The brothers got ready to run while Drake counted. "One . . . two . . . three!"

Josh opened the door and they ran into the living room. Tiberius was immediately in their faces, barking viciously. Drake and Josh ran in circles, screaming their heads off, while Stan cowered in the bathroom.

Tiberius chased Drake, then Josh, then Drake again. Tiberius was right on Drake's heels, and Josh was able to get to the front door. Drake stood on the coffee table and leaped. But instead of landing near the door, as he hoped, he found himself hanging from Mrs. Hayfer's ceiling fan. Tiberius nipped at his sneakers.

"Josh! Help! Josh!" Drake screamed. He tried not to spin and make himself dizzy, but the fan had a mind of its own. He couldn't let go without dropping down right into the dog's jaws. "I'm dangling and rotating!" he yelled. "Josh, help!"

Josh opened the front door again and peeked in. What he wanted to do more than anything was run away, but Drake needed him. He had an idea. "Hang on, Drake," he yelled, dashing across the living room and through another door.

Josh barely made it — shutting the door just as Tiberius reached it. The dog turned his attention back to Drake.

Drake was desperate. He couldn't hold on much longer, and the minute he fell, Tiberius would sink sharp teeth into his soft skin. "Josh! Josh, where'd you go?"

"I'm in the kitchen," Josh yelled.

"This is no time for snacking!" Drake said, trying to get a better grip.

Josh had found what he was looking for. He burst back into the living room waving a raw steak in the air. "Look, Tiberius! Meat!" he said, running over to the window.

Josh opened the window and threw the steak into the front yard. Tiberius barked, ran, and jumped out the window after the steak.

"Ha! Sucker!" Josh yelled. Then he ran over to Drake. "Okay, Drake. Come down."

Drake threw one leg over Josh's shoulder. Josh staggered around, trying to put his brother down gently, but Drake landed on the floor with a thud.

"Is he gone?" Drake asked.

"He's gone!" Josh said with a huge grin.

Normally Drake would give his brother a high five, but this rescue deserved something more. "Oh, hug me, brothah," Drake answered, throwing his arms wide.

The guys shared a victory hug. Relieved and exhausted. They had battled the beast and they had won.

Or had they?

Suddenly Tiberius ran through the front door. It seemed like the steak had only given him a taste for more meat. He eyed the brothers, barking just as viciously as he had before.

Drake and Josh screamed and scanned the room. They definitely didn't want to go back to the powder room, and Tiberius and his big teeth were blocking the front door. Drake took a flying dive out of the open front window, followed by his brother.

CHAPTER SIX

Drake and Josh didn't stop running until they were safe inside their own home with the front door closed and locked behind them. Josh jumped over the back of the couch and landed on the cushions.

"And we are home!" he said, huffing and puffing.

Drake stopped to hug a lamp. He had never been so happy to be home in his entire life. "I love this house," he said.

"Me too, bro," Josh agreed, still out of breath from their mad dash to safely. "That was insane!"

"I have never been so scared in my whole life," Drake admitted.

"I know, right?" Josh said, finally catching his breath. "We better tell Dad what happened."

"Yeah," Drake agreed.

Josh stood and looked around. The fancy exercise machine was empty. "Dad?" he called.

"Hey, Walter?" Drake yelled.

"Pop?"

"I wonder where he went," Drake said.

Josh was too tired to worry about it right then. He shrugged and dropped back onto the couch.

Meanwhile, Walter Nichols had begun to worry about the guys. He jogged over to Mrs. Hayfer's house as part of his new training program. He found the front door wide open.

"Hello?" he called, walking across the living room. "Drake? Josh?"

"Hello? Who's that?" Stan called back from the powder room.

Mr. Nichols opened the door and poked his head inside. Stan was still sitting on the toilet. There was a pile of soap shavings around his feet.

"What's up?" Stan asked.

"Hello," Mr. Nichols said, growing more confused by the second.

Stan held up his bright yellow carving. "I made a duck."

Mr. Nichols was more than a little creeped out by

a strange man in the bathroom making soap animals. He closed the door without a word and stepped back into the living room.

"Drake? Josh?" he called again.

Tiberius had lost the boys when they jumped over a fence and headed back home again. At that moment he padded through the front door. He stopped short when he saw Mr. Nichols.

"Hey," Mr. Nichols said.

But Tiberius didn't like Walter Nichols any more than he liked his sons. He had a fierce expression, even before he started barking.

Mr. Nichols screamed in terror and ran around the living room with Tiberius snapping at him. "No, nice doggie," he screamed.

But Tiberius wasn't a nice doggie. He was a ferocious man-eater. Mr. Nichols raced for the front door with Tiberius right behind him, snapping at his heels all the way home.

Drake and Josh were finally relaxed enough to sit down and watch some TV. They popped a big bowl of popcorn and put their feet up on the coffee table.

Drake was still mulling over a question he had earlier in the day. "So why do they call it *New* Jersey if they never even had an *old* Jersey?"

"I don't know," Josh answered. "I wasn't at the meeting." Did he look like he was from one of the thirteen original colonies? "Hey, turn it to channel five," he said. "I'm going to go grab a drink."

Josh headed into the kitchen while Drake changed the channel and raised the volume with the remote.

Mr. Nichols's screams blended in with the noise coming from the television as he ran through the front door, across the room behind Drake, and out the side door into the backyard. Tiberius barked at his heels.

Drake looked over his shoulder and shook his head. There was nothing there, so why was he still hearing a dog bark?

Josh came back with his drink and dropped onto the couch again.

"So," Drake said. "Is there an old Hampshire?"

Josh said nothing. He didn't even take his eyes off the television. He simply picked up the popcorn bowl and turned it upside down on Drake's head.